# Majesty
## *from* Assateague

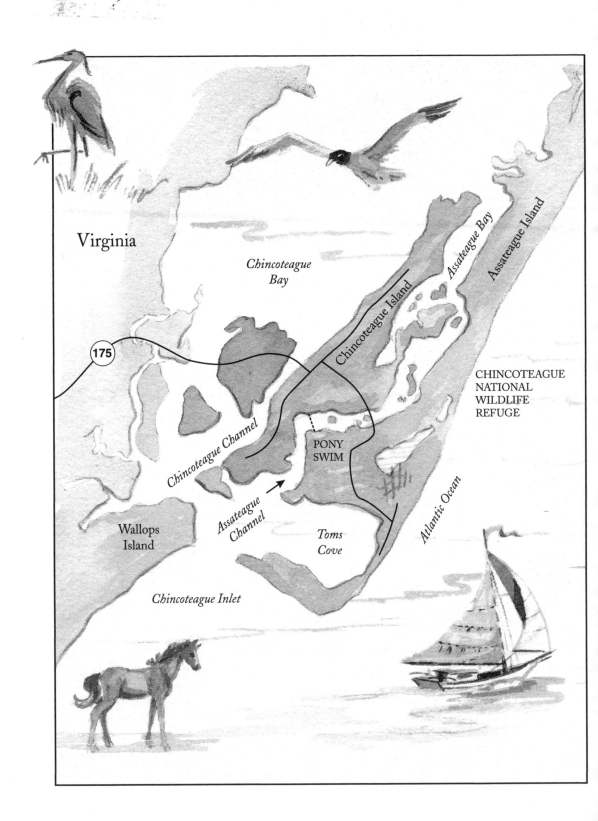

Virginia

Chincoteague
Bay

175

Chincoteague Channel

Wallops
Island

Assateague
Channel

Chincoteague Island

Assateague Bay

Assateague Island

CHINCOTEAGUE
NATIONAL
WILDLIFE
REFUGE

PONY
SWIM

Toms
Cove

Atlantic Ocean

Chincoteague Inlet

# *Majesty from Assateague*

HARVEY HAGMAN
illustrated by DAVID AIKEN

Tidewater Publishers
Centreville, Maryland

To pony lovers everywhere and to my favorite pony lover, my wife.

—H. H.

Library of Congress Cataloging-in-Publication Data

Hagman, Harvey Dixon, 1939–
   Majesty from Assateague / Harvey Hagman ; illustrated by David
Aiken.—1st Tidewater Publishers ed.
         p. cm.
Summary: After being orphaned and injured in a car crash, Michael goes
to live with his grandparents who encourage his dream of acquiring a
special horse he first sees on Assateague Island.
   ISBN 0-87033-552-9 (Paperback)
[1. Orphans—Fiction. 2. Chincoteague pony—Fiction. 3.
Ponies—Fiction. 4. People with disabilities—Fiction. 5.
Grandfathers—Fiction.] I. Aiken, David, 1940– ill. II. Title.
PZ7.H12456Maj 2003
[Fic]—dc22                                    2003019431

Manufactured in the United States of America
First Tidewater Publishers edition, 2003

# Majesty
## from Assateague

Puffy clouds floated lazily through a rich blue sky. Below the vast expanse of blue, the surf lapped white foam against the sandy shore, and thin beach grass swayed on the dunes. A breeze ruffled Morning Star's mane as the wind shifted.

Morning Star, a fine figure of a pony with a diamond-shaped star on her forehead, whinnied in a gentle, contented way. It was a perfect day for her to give birth and the place was perfect too— the island of Assateague, a shifting strip of barrier beach that gave way to salt marshes, great ponds, and pine forests.

The sturdy mare with a shaggy, deep brown coat belonged to the band, or harem, of the stallion Bright Star. His harem was composed of about fifteen mares and their frolicking offspring. Bright Star was gentle as he moved among his band, but he could be wild when challenged by a marauding stallion—rearing, biting, and kicking wildly with his powerful hooves.

As Morning Star grazed, the day slowly changed. The wind picked up, clouds formed and blacked out the sun, and the sea began to roar. A powerful northeaster, stormy winds out of the northeast, pushed down the coast and lashed the island. At the height of the storm a shaft of brilliant sunshine pierced the clouds and shone on the dark, silvery seas. At that moment Morning Star left the band, trotted off by herself, and in a few minutes felt herself giving birth. As a cool breath of wind passed over her she heard a low neigh. She had given birth to a beautiful pony.

Morning Star licked her new foal as the two rested on the ground. They stared at each other and exchanged knowing neighs. Exhausted, Morning Star looked up contentedly at the heavens and thought, "I'll call her Majesty, after this majestic scene of sky and sea."

Majesty struggled to stand several times, but her shaky legs could not yet support her, and she fell each time. Finally, she managed to stay upright and with uncertain steps began to follow Morning Star as she grazed. Her father, the stallion Bright Star, kept a watchful eye on his new daughter. Later, Majesty nuzzled her mother's belly and enjoyed her first mother's milk. As the days passed, she continued to suckle and felt herself filling with energy.

Spring gave way to summer and the band followed the stallion Bright Star, feeding on coarse saltmarsh cordgrass, beach grass, and sometimes thorny greenbrier, bayberry twigs, rose hips, seaweed, and even poison ivy. Bright Star loved eating greenbrier, the climbing woody vines with prickly stems, oval leaves, and blue-black berries.

At night the band rested under velvet skies sprinkled with a million twinkling stars. Mornings broke over the ocean in soft pearls and pinks, and with the warm breezes of summer, Majesty grew in strength and love of the harem.

Now she nibbled more grass and sought out Morning Star for milk less often. Sometimes she nibbled grass in the shadow of Bright Star, other times she rubbed against her mother, who nuzzled her in a loving way.

This peaceful rhythm of life continued for months until one day Majesty's keen nose picked up the scent of the young marauding stallion Devil Chaser, who was full of energy and high spirits. Devil Chaser had a reddish-brown coat, and his muscles stood out when he was excited.

Bright Star moved quickly between his band and the attacking stallion and drove the surprised mares and foals away at a gallop. Devil Chaser watched the harem's movements, then his mane flew in the wind as he approached and challenged Bright Star.

The stallions eyed each other. They moved closer, necks arched and tails high, each sizing up the opponent as they trotted back and forth, side by side. Suddenly, Devil Chaser lunged at the older stallion's neck and drove his teeth into Bright Star's flesh. Bright Star retaliated, sinking his teeth into Devil Chaser's shoulder.

Then Bright Star's hoof stuck in a hole and he tripped, causing him to lose his grip. As he recovered his balance, a panting Devil Chaser raced back at him, biting him on the shoulder, flank, and leg.

Majesty inched closer to watch the fierce combat, stunned by the stallions' violence.

The harem had been Bright Star's for many years. As a young stallion he had driven off an aging stallion. Under him the harem had grown and prospered as he guided it from one grazing ground to another. Now he was the aging stallion.

Bright Star thought somehow he must find the strength to combat this young stallion. He threw off Devil Chaser's attack and retreated; bloody and in pain, he let out a screaming whinny. He trotted back toward the young stallion. They reared and their hooves pawed the air wildly, but no blows were landed. As they crashed together, Devil Chaser dropped his head and once more sank his teeth deep into Bright Star's neck.

Bright Star retreated in anguish and shook his head in disbelief. With his last energy, he charged Devil Chaser and drove his teeth into the retreating horse's side, then viciously bit his neck. Devil Chaser broke off the fight, but by that time, blood was running into Bright Star's eyes and down his mane. He staggered, and his head hung low. His vision blurred, and he saw stars.

Majesty felt baffled. Earlier, she was certain her father would win easily. Now she wasn't so sure. The fierce battle frightened her, but she felt her own anger rising, expanding her blood vessels. She would make Devil Chaser pay for attacking her father. But how? She didn't know. This stallion was twice her size.

Suddenly both ponies charged and landed their hooves on their opponent's head. Devil Chaser's head swam, everything

went black as he fell backward. Stars flashed before his eyes. "This old stallion is a worthy opponent," he thought.

With the strength of youth, the young stallion charged again, and this time his hind legs delivered two stunning blows. Crack! Crack!

Moments earlier, Majesty had realized her father was finished. Instinctively she raced forward between the battling horses and reared high in the air. For a split second, she looked directly into the shimmering sun and its brightness blinded her. Then she heard the deafening cracks and felt two frightful blows as her body fell to the ground. Her consciousness faded. Everything went black before her eyes. She tried to move her legs, her head, her ears. Nothing responded.

A vision formed in the blackness. "Am I dreaming?" she wondered. She blinked her eyes and saw ponies working in a mine deep within the high, rugged Andes mountains of South America. Snow glistened on the towering peaks, and water ran down the mountainside into the high valleys. But the ponies saw little of this splendor. Their lives were spent in darkness, their muscles straining to haul wagons of ore to the surface, where it would be processed and turned into precious metal.

As the ponies worked day after day, they began to lose their eyesight because of the dust and darkness. Their world grew fainter and darker, until their sight finally disappeared. Still they strained and pulled. They ate so they could continue to work and they slept so their muscles could recover to work the following day. But one day their routine was interrupted when twenty foals were taken from their mothers and herded aboard an ancient ship. Its timbers creaked and its canvas sails were ragged.

Under the yellow sun and turquoise sky of Peru, the ship's bow and stern lines were released and it rode out from the harbor. As its aging sails caught the wind, it headed north. At Panama, the ponies joyously felt the earth under their hooves, and they recovered from the tossing seas. After crossing the steaming swamps and sweltering jungles of Central America, the ponies boarded another ship. Their nostrils again filled with the fresh smell of salt air.

With fair winds and pleasantly rolling seas, the ship cruised the Caribbean, circled the Florida Keys, and made its way northward, riding the gentle swells of the Atlantic. The journey went well until the coast of Virginia came into view off the port side. Above it, black clouds piled up over the flat land. The seas began to toss as the winds rose. Waves washed the slippery deck, and the ponies became nervous. They began to slide back and forth as the deck pitched and the rain beat down.

A vicious wave caught the ship and threw it on its side. Fear blazed in the sailors' eyes as the captain spun the wheel. The sails stretched, and the bow plunged beneath a wave. The ship righted itself as a monster wave rose on the horizon and raced toward the vessel. Once more the captain swung the wheel to turn the ship into the wave, but this time it was too late.

Water swept the deck and flooded it. A huge wave lifted the ponies and floated them overboard, washing them effortlessly into a turbulent sea. The ponies fought to keep their heads above the water as they began to swim slowly toward shore.

In the lead swam a black colt called Black Thunder. He seemed to sense a way to use the swelling seas to help the herd get to the land.

As the lightning flashed, Black Thunder turned and looked back at the ship. With a deafening crack its two masts splintered. The bow pitched skyward and the ship slowly slid backward into the sea. In the blink of an eye, the ship and its crew disappeared in the howling storm.

Black Thunder's muscles ached as he swam toward the shore, at last riding the swift surf onto the beach. The herd followed, each pony fighting for balance until its hooves found the soft sand. Despite his exhaustion, an exhilaration filled Black Thunder as he looked out upon Assateague Island. Freedom! Freedom to live peacefully on this land, sharing the wilderness with other wild creatures.

The other ponies struggled up on the beach behind Black Thunder, eager to follow him to the safety of the island and to wait for the winds to die down, the seas to calm, and the sun to return.

Then Majesty heard Black Thunder speak to her. "I am your ancestor. I led the herd to this beautiful place which you call home. We learned to survive the rigors of island life in all seasons. With the cattle egrets to help us in our battle against the biting flies and ticks, we have lived in harmony with the other creatures of this majestic place. Now the island has passed on to you.

"Fight as we fought. Do not let your life slip away. You have a destiny to fulfill. So live. Let your strength return. Fight on."

Michael Jenning's soccer team had pulled out its last three games in the final minutes of play. The championship game was hours away. Michael's father George swung the steering wheel sharply into a left-hand turn en route to the soccer field.

Michael's mother Donna, seated beside George in the front seat, turned toward Michael, who was pulling on his tennis shoes in the back seat, and said, "I know that you're fast, Michael. You've scored more goals than any other ten-year-old in the league. But pass the ball off more."

"I will, Mom," said Michael. "Just watch. I can't wait for the game. We'll win the championship. We've beaten this team before. We'll do it again."

His mother smiled. "I know you will."

Later, a woman a block away from the accident said, "I thought a bomb had gone off. It was that loud."

In the hospital's intensive care ward, the doctor turned to the nurse and said, "How many days has he been in the coma now?"

"Ten, counting the night of the accident."

"Any changes?"

Michael's eyes slowly opened, then blinked shut. "Doctor, I thought I saw his eyes move," said the nurse.

The doctor bent over Michael, his face inches away. "Can you hear me, son?"

"I . . ." Michael's lips were so dry he could barely whisper. "Where am I?" Michael heard the voice, but it sounded like it was coming from the next room, and it was far too weak to be his.

Two weeks later, Michael rested flat on his back in the hospital bed as his grandmother and grandfather told him the bad news. They recounted the terrible automobile crash and the tragic death of his parents.

"They felt no pain, Michael," said his grandmother. "It was too quick." She went into great detail about how the medics found him. She described his hospital stay, his crushed legs, and his head injuries. She explained how the doctors had saved him, how the championship soccer game was canceled, and how everyone prayed for his recovery. He dozed off twice as the words flooded out.

It was too much to figure out. Michael felt like it was all a dream, the whole, terrible, confusing mess. And here he was in a hospital bed, barely able to move, much less walk.

When his grandparents left the room, Michael felt alone and cried for the first time. He wanted to forget everything. Sleep was peaceful, understandable. Life wasn't.

Weeks later Michael was fitted with leg braces and given a pair of crutches. When he left the hospital he would have fallen getting into the wheelchair if the nurse and his grandpa hadn't grabbed him.

He started calling his grandparents Grams and Gramps. Now they were his acting mom and dad, and the three lived in his parents' home, the place where he had grown up. That was comforting.

Walking was difficult. School was difficult, and watching the soccer team brought tears to his eyes so he quit doing that. It was particularly hard as he watched his old teammates drift away and realized that his memories of his parents were slowly fading.

One weekend after his physical therapy he asked Grams, "Mom used to ride horses, didn't she?"

"She became an excellent rider over the years. When she was your age she was a good beginning rider."

"I want to do something to remember her. When I'm better, maybe I'll take riding lessons, too."

"Your mother would like that, I'm sure."

One day, Gramps decided to take the family for a ride. The car headed east, continued for some hours, then crossed the long causeway leading to Chincoteague Island, off the Virginia portion of the Delmarva Peninsula. Grams and Michael looked out on the vast expanse of marsh and sea. Soon the car passed through the town, crossed another bridge, wound through the wildlife refuge, and came to a stop at Assateague Island beach.

Michael felt stronger but still walked haltingly with crutches. The doctors told him he was lucky to walk at all. He tried to be glad about that, but running across a soccer field full speed to kick a goal was not easy to forget. And he couldn't forget it. It kept flashing across his mind.

"What are you thinking about?" Gramps asked as the two walked along the beach while Grams rested in the car.

"My crutches sink in the sand. Can we walk slower?"

"Sure, anything you say. Look at those ponies on the dunes up ahead."

"Wow! Wild ponies."

"Yes, they're the wild Assateague ponies. Those on the Virginia side are called Chincoteague ponies. They've adapted to their meager food supply—they look happy enough."

"Sure do," said Michael, his eyes getting a distant, excited look.

"Their life is fairly simple. They travel their range, feeding and resting. A stallion has a harem or band of mares. Sometimes stallions that have no mares band together."

"Bachelor bands?"

"Yep. Sometimes a young male may attempt to steal mares from other bands. He cuts a mare off from a group and drives her away. If he gets away with it, he starts his own harem."

"Does another stallion then try to take his mares?"

"Sure. It's nature's way of preventing inbreeding."

"Inbreeding?"

"That's when too many animals or people have the same parents or relatives, Michael."

"What else do the ponies do, Gramps?"

"Sometimes young females leave their harems and wander around until they find another band or a bachelor stallion."

As Gramps spoke, the head of a pony appeared behind a dune. Majesty looked out across the lonely beach where a light surf broke. The old man walked easily along the sea, the pony thought, but the young boy moved slowly. He looked like he had four ungainly legs.

Majesty thought that she would show him how easy it is to run on four legs. She raced over the dunes toward the sea. Then she wheeled and galloped past the man and boy, her mane flying, her hooves barely touching the ground, a symphony of motion and grace. Before they knew it she had passed the two walkers, turned, and disappeared over the dunes.

"I'll be darned," said Gramps. "Never saw anything like that. That pony ran right at us. It had a lot of spunk. It was almost like that pony wanted to show off for us."

"I think the pony wanted to show us how wonderful it is to run and be free, free as the wind," said Michael. "It made me remember how much fun it was to run, dribbling the soccer ball while everyone tried to catch me. It makes me want to work harder now at trying to walk without crutches."

Michael tossed his crutches to Gramps. He took a couple of halting steps, lost his balance in the sand, and fell. For a moment Michael lay motionless, then suddenly he burst out laughing.

Gramps was relieved; he feared Michael was going to cry. He laughed too, helped Michael back to his feet, and handed him his crutches.

"That pony gave me hope, Gramps. I know I won't walk with crutches forever," said Michael. "I can feel myself getting stronger."

"Your parents would be proud of you, Michael," said Gramps, "I know I am."

"Thanks, Gramps."

Majesty continued to grow, spending about eighteen hours a day eating. She would wrap her lips around the tough saltmarsh cordgrass, grab it between her strong teeth, and rip it from the earth with her powerful jaws. Then her molars, the teeth she used for grinding, would pulverize the tasty grass and she would swallow it.

She learned to deal with the pesky horseflies, mosquitoes, and ticks, rubbing against trees and snapping at the pests with her teeth as Morning Star often did. She rolled on the ground, hoping the friendly cattle egrets would feast off the flies and mosquitoes on her legs and belly.

The days slid past as Majesty galloped to and fro among the mares while other colts chased her in and out. She would fight playfully, nipping with her teeth at another foal's mane, rearing high, then wheeling and kicking with her hind feet. When she tired, she napped on the soft earth.

But she never strayed far from Morning Star, even when her mother nudged her away or playfully nipped her on the neck. Sometimes she remembered Bright Star, the valiant stallion who fathered her and died battling with Devil Chaser. The scar remained where Devil Chaser's hoof had crashed into her skull. But it seemed so long ago. Devil Chaser had never driven her from his harem, but she usually found herself grazing far from the stallion. And he never mated with Morning Star.

Morning Star had one very bad habit. She would wander close to the ocean when she sensed a storm coming. Sometimes, any excuse would serve to bring her into the surf—the heat, the bugs, or just boredom. At first, Devil Chaser would prick up his ears and lower his head to drive her back into the harem, but slowly he gave up, letting her wander into the surf at will.

One day Morning Star headed into the surf as the sky darkened and the wind shifted and blew fiercely. Majesty followed her mother into the shallows, but the pounding of the waves frightened her and she retreated toward the shore. Even in the shallows she had trouble standing as the surf surged in.

Far out to sea she could see a huge wave building, a wall of water that pushed everything before it as it rushed toward the shore. Although it was a long way off, she whinnied loudly to alert Morning Star. The mare was tossing her head back and forth in the roaring surf, playing like a foal enjoying its first dip in the ocean. She was never more fearless or playful than when she was running about in a storm.

Majesty nickered, a low-pitched whinny, but it was lost in the roar of the surf. She nickered again, then let out a whinnied scream. Morning Star heard it and turned her head toward Majesty. But she was already lost in the storm's power and fury. She felt she was a part of the storm, not threatened by it.

As Majesty watched, the giant wave washed over Morning Star and she disappeared as it swept toward the shore. A moment later Majesty saw Morning Star's head rise above the water as the wave rushed toward her. Majesty felt her body pitched skyward, cartwheeling with her hooves flying above her head, a feeling of exhilaration filling her. She thought this must be how a bird feels as it rides the wind.

But then she was slammed onto the sand, landing on her side. The wave knocked the wind from her lungs, like a giant punch. Gasping for breath, she felt an irresistible pull drawing her out to sea. Surrounded by the swirling water, she got a quick breath through her nostrils, then another, before she was pulled under again. Her nostrils, then her lungs, filled with water. In a desperate fight for life, she kicked valiantly as she battled her way back toward the beach. Her lungs screamed for air. Air. Air! She scrambled to her feet and raced out of the surf.

Far out to sea, the ocean was tossing Morning Star about like a rag doll, her legs tumbling over her head again and again. Then her head popped above the water, the waves widened, and she found herself between the crests, exhausted but breathing easily. She could not feel any broken bones. But now she was too far out.

Majesty galloped up and down the beach, searching for her mother in the waves. The giant wave had disappeared, but the storm still raged and the surf still pounded. She turned back toward the island and saw Devil Chaser looking calmly out to sea. Majesty let out a whinnied scream for help. The stallion turned and trotted off behind a dune, unconcerned.

This enraged Majesty. She galloped into the waves again. She could still see Morning Star's head bobbing between the waves, appearing, then disappearing. Each time she feared she would not see her mother's head again. She kicked furiously, straining to get beyond the pull of the surf, feeling her strength slowly disappear in the tossing sea. She told herself, "I will not fail this time. I will not black out."

She rested, floating for a moment to regain her breath. Then she turned her head in the direction she had last seen Morning Star. Their eyes met. The mare seemed to be smiling in the raging sea. Morning Star seemed to be saying, "It's all right. I was foolish. But this is a wonderful way to die. I am at peace. Save yourself. Live on."

As the young pony watched, Morning Star disappeared beneath the waves. Majesty kept swimming and searching but

she did not see her mother again. Slowly, she swam back to the beach, and galloped out of the surf. Then she collapsed far up on the beach.

Majesty did not know whether she lost consciousness or fell into a deep sleep. When she awoke, stars twinkled overhead. She rose, shook herself, and trotted off to join the harem. She was now alone—alone in the night, in the morning, and in all the days ahead.

One morning, Michael finished breakfast from the tray Gramps had brought. He was about to grab his crutches and head for the kitchen when Grams came in.

"Michael, you've got to concentrate on learning to walk again. For now, practice until you can use these crutches well. Then maybe someday you'll walk without them."

"OK, Grams. Thanks."

Later, she told Gramps, "Time will tell whether he'll ever walk again, but we've got to find something that will take Michael's mind off soccer and also burn up some of that boy's energy."

"He loves those ponies at Assateague. Let's take him to pony penning at Chincoteague next July," said Gramps. "Meanwhile, I'll take him down there fishing. He doesn't have to walk to fish."

The fishing boat *Reel Time* moved across a calm ocean, slowly making its way back to Chincoteague after a pleasant, sunny day. Michael and Gramps had reeled in bluefish, sea trout, and even a couple of rockfish. Both were bronzed from the sun and weary but happy. They had munched egg-salad sandwiches and lukewarm hamburgers, nibbled on potato chips, and enjoyed a lot of sodas.

"This was really a cool day, Gramps," Michael said.

"Great time!" said Gramps. "We'll do it again."

"Can the boat run along the coast so I can look for ponies?" Michael asked.

The captain obligingly changed course to follow the shore of Assateague. Michael peered through binoculars while leaning on his crutches as the bow of *Reel Time* rose and fell on the swells. Gramps supported him. Michael spotted osprey, or fish hawks, diving after their supper, and pelicans making splashy attacks to get their catch, but he could see no ponies prancing along the beach, no harems moving across the marsh behind the dunes.

When the captain observed Michael's interest in ponies, he told him above the motor's roar, "If you like ponies, you'll love the pony penning."

"Pony penning? What's that?"

"Well it all began hundreds of years ago, when unclaimed horses and other livestock were rounded up and branded by early colonists. It was really a party, with feasting, music, maybe some dancing. It was a lot of fun for all.

"Years later the first modern pony penning was held—in 1924 to be exact. It raised money for our Chincoteague Volunteer Fire Company. Every year it's held in July, starting on the last Wednesday of the month.

"We call the guys who round up the ponies 'saltwater cowboys.' They herd the ponies across the channel on Wednesday before thousands of people who come to see them. Most of the foals and yearlings are auctioned off on Thursday.

"The new owners must provide safe transportation and good homes for their new ponies. Most foals are easily tamed and adapt well to domestic life. Those ponies that are not sold swim back to Assateague in the following days. That's great fun to watch, too. The whole thing is a great show. And everyone loves the ponies."

"You mean anyone can buy one?" asked Michael.

"All you need is the money. But it is a lot of money for a boy your age."

"Boy, would that be a thrill to have a pony!"

"Well, you never know. Maybe someday you'll own your own pony."

Michael thought this over. But how could he get the money? Gramps and Grams did not have enough money to purchase a pony. Neither did he.

After the boat docked, Grams joined the two fishermen. The trio walked slowly down the island's lonely roads and searched the salt marsh, but this day they saw no sign of ponies.

Majesty was just getting over the shock of her mother's death when she began to feel woozy. A swarm of pesky mosquitoes had landed on her back one day, bit her fiercely, and disappeared. She didn't know it, but she had contracted swamp fever from the mosquitoes. She felt feverish, had chills, and finally lost so much strength she could not stand.

When Gramps, Grams, and Michael hiked the road nearby, they couldn't see her. Majesty lay suffering in the marsh grass, tossing weakly, kicking her hooves aimlessly in the air, trying to stop her head from spinning and make her stomach pains ease.

The ground was warm, and the sunlight offered some comfort, but Majesty feared she might lie there forever. Then the dream returned. Her ancestor Black Thunder pawed the ancient earth and said, "Not yet, Majesty. It's not your time yet." But Majesty's mind drifted in the heat: she thought, "Now I can join Morning Star and Bright Star and this pain will leave me."

Her dream returned. Black Thunder repeated his warning: "You still have things to accomplish. Stand up and walk. You must eat."

Majesty struggled to her feet. She forced herself to begin munching on the beach grass. Days later her head began to clear, even though she still tired quickly. But now she knew she would not die. Days passed and her strength increased. When the biting flies bothered her, she stamped her feet angrily or snapped at them with her old speed and strength.

As Michael was leaving the town of Chincoteague, he noticed that many of the shops sold beautiful paintings of ponies. After he returned home, he found books with pictures of horses and

drew them to look like Chincoteague ponies. It was harder than he thought it would be.

But his sketches improved as he drew hundreds of Chincoteague ponies. Grams bought him a drawing board. The school art teacher, Mr. Walters, offered tips and loaned him some oil paints. "When you finish three good oil paintings, bring them to me," he said. "I've got an idea."

Michael picked his best sketches, painted them in oils, and brought his three favorite paintings to the teacher after school. He was nervous. Maybe Mr. Walters wouldn't like any of them.

The teacher welcomed him warmly and immediately examined the paintings. There was a long silence, then finally he spoke. "These are all good, but I do have a suggestion," he said.

Michael's heart fell. After all his work, the teacher didn't seem to like any of them. "What?" he said, trying not to sound hurt.

"Why don't you take the grouping from your first painting, use the background from the second, and the colors from the third?"

"Don't you like any of them?" Michael asked, disheartened.

"I like them all, at least parts of them all," answered the teacher. "Just combine them. What do you think?"

Michael studied his three paintings. He hated to agree, but Mr. Walters was right. He'd have to start over. "But before I start again, tell me your idea," said Michael.

"It's this," replied the teacher. "Do one more painting that we both like. Then I'll take it to a friend and have colored prints made. He offers a good price for three hundred prints. Then you can sell the prints."

"Wow, what a great idea," Michael said. "I thought I was going to have to do hundreds of paintings. What a relief."

Michael was so happy he felt like running out to the playground to kick a soccer ball. Instead he grabbed his crutches and swung himself out of the room, yelling, "Whoopee, thanks a lot."

When he was finished with the final painting, Michael showed it to Mr. Walters and held his breath. The teacher walked up to it, backed away, then came right up next to it, his eyes examining every detail.

"I think it's perfect," the teacher said. "I'll bring the three hundred prints to you in about a week. I'll pay my friend and you pay me as you sell them."

"Cool. That's so cool! Thanks!" Michael said.

Michael figured he could never sell all three hundred prints himself, so he came up with a plan. He would ask a local Girl Scout troop to sell eighty as a way to raise money. He would make the same deal with a local Cub Scout troop, with his grandma's bridge club, and with grandpa's bowling team.

His former soccer team took ninety of the prints right away, more than he had offered. His old coach said the team would sell them as a fund-raiser. Michael wound up asking his art teacher for more prints so he would have some to sell!

On the morning of the scheduled pony penning, Gramps woke Michael at 4:30 A.M. The stars twinkled dimly as Gramps drove the car, with a sea kayak on the cartop carrier, to a parking lot on the Assateague channel. Gramps hoped that someone would be around to help him launch the kayak and prayed that Michael could get in without incident. Michael improved every time they practiced. He only tipped the kayak once. Though sopping wet, they both had a good laugh.

Gramps parked the car. He gave another kayaker a yell and the two slipped the kayak easily into the water as the luminous pink and pearl dawn spread across the horizon. Michael strapped on his life jacket. He adjusted his sturdy Christmas knife in its sheath. Just in case. Just in case of what he wasn't sure, but he wanted to be prepared.

He settled himself expertly into the sea kayak, then held onto the dock. Gramps handed him his paddle. He loaded the cold thermos, the sandwiches, and the camera in its waterproof bag, and they pushed off.

"We're early, just enjoy the sunrise and paddle slowly," Gramps said. "Are you comfortable up front?"

"Great! You did all the work, Gramps."

As he paddled Michael thought about what he would see. Some 150 ponies would swim from the marshes of Assateague to Memorial Park on Chincoteague. Already he could see a crowd of people gathering in the park and along the shore. The ponies would swim in an area called pony-swim lane. They would swim at slack tide, sometime between 7 and 11 in the morning. He hoped it would be early, because it was already getting warm. He stopped paddling when he saw a rope in the water blocking the way.

"Can't go any farther, Gramps."

"OK. How about some breakfast?"

"Great! I'm starved," Michael said.

Gramps passed him a sandwich on his paddle and Michael turned around to lift the thermos. The kayak swayed under the shifting weight, nearly tipped, and righted itself after Gramps quickly put out his paddle to stop the roll.

"Whoa there, big fellow," Gramps said, laughing.

"Sorry, I'll be more careful."

Far across the marsh Michael could see the saltwater cowboys, members of the Volunteer Fire Company. They were dressed in their traditional baseball hats and wore knee-high boots as they tried to herd the ponies together.

Ropes were swung, and shouts were echoing through the marsh as the ponies began to move toward the channel. The sun climbed higher in the sky as ponies from all the harems were banded together—foals, yearlings, mares, and stallions. In these close quarters, the stallions began to get restless. Two battles broke out before the saltwater cowboys could separate the rearing stallions. Devil Chaser looked nervous and whinnied a high screaming challenge, but before he could act a cowboy trotted his horse in front of him and slapped him with his reins.

Suddenly, a red flare shot into the morning sky, sending a streaming crimson arc against the blue sky. The swim had officially begun. Amid yells, shouts, and the cracks of whips, the herd was driven into the muddy shallows. About a quarter-mile of water spread before them. Majesty found herself pushed to the outside of the pack. Her hooves sank into the mud as she moved forward. The cool water was refreshing.

Soon the muddy bottom fell away and the ponies began to swim. Only their bobbing heads were visible, ears upright and pointed forward.

Majesty swam easily, effortlessly. But suddenly one of her front hooves became entangled, then the other one. She kicked harder, but could not free her legs. She found herself sinking. "Seaweed is usually easy to kick off," she thought. "I wonder what's happening?"

"That pony swimming toward us is in trouble, Gramps," Michael shouted.

"Keep calm, everything will be all right," Gramps said.

"She's swimming hard, but her head's going under," yelled Michael.

Majesty fell farther behind the herd as the ponies swam slowly, making their way toward Memorial Park. The press boat tossed off a light wake as it came out to position its photographers. A helicopter carrying a television crew whirred overhead.

Majesty's nostrils filled with water as she fought to bring her head above water. She let out a screaming neigh for help. "Paddle, Gramps. That pony is in trouble," Michael shouted. The kayak lurched forward toward the pony before Gramps could stroke. But he pulled hard on the second stroke.

Majesty was in a battle for her life, but she could not kick herself free. Her head went under again. Alarmed, a saltwater cowboy guided his horse toward her.

As the kayak knifed through the water toward the struggling Majesty, Michael saw the problem—her legs were tangled in monofilament fishline. He pulled his knife from its sheath and dove into the water. Confused, Majesty turned to swim away from him, but she couldn't.

Michael grabbed Majesty's tail and pulled himself toward her. Then he accidentally dropped his knife. How could he free the pony's flailing legs? He lifted his legs and pushed down on the monofilament line with his feet. The water swirled around him as Majesty thrashed back and forth. Michael felt his tennis shoes hit the muddy bottom. He felt Majesty swing her hind legs away from him, free of the line.

Now the line was caught on his tennis shoes, and he reached down to free himself. A rapid jerk freed his feet, but he was upside down or sideways, he wasn't sure. His lungs screamed for air. Then suddenly powerful teeth closed on his shirt collar, and he felt his body pulled to the surface. He gasped for air and looked at Majesty's powerful jaws inches away.

Michael was flabbergasted. Majesty was surprised. They stared at each other for a brief second. Who saved who?

Though exhausted, Majesty swam freely now. She turned and swam back toward the herd. Michael went down again but his head bobbed up quickly. Gramps maneuvered the kayak toward him and held out his paddle. "Grab it."

Michael weakly grabbed the paddle and Gramps pulled him toward the bow of the kayak. "Throw yourself over the bow and hang on," Gramps commanded. Michael's tired muscles grabbed the kayak and he hung on.

Michael thought, "I couldn't do that again. That was one lucky dive."

He reached for his knife, but then he remembered it was gone.

"I lost my knife, Gramps," he said. "But I saved that pony."

"Yes, I think you did. Then, that pony saved you. Can you hang on until I paddle us over to that log?"

"I'll try."

"We'll get you back aboard there," Gramps said.

Michael was glad the log wasn't far away. When he got there, Gramps jumped over the side and lifted him back into his seat. Michael's muscles trembled.

"Fine job, son. I'm proud of you. You saved that pony's life."

"That's the same pony I saw running on the beach after my accident," said Michael. "She's a beauty. I'm going to bid on her at the auction."

As the two spoke the first pony clambered ashore at Memorial Park. This lucky pony would be called King or Queen Neptune and would be given away at the carnival that afternoon. The crowd cheered as the rest of the group splashed out of the water and came ashore.

The herd rested for twenty or thirty minutes amid the admiration of the crowd. Then, led by a truck and herded by saltwater cowboys, the ponies walked down Main Street to the carnival grounds. People lined the way. Small children pointed out their favorite ponies. Waves and cheers greeted the ponies.

Michael took a long nap that afternoon. Gramps dozed off for a while too. They awoke with big appetites, had a hearty fish dinner, and went to the corral in the carnival grounds where the ponies were penned. Michael spotted Majesty through the fence. She stood quietly with the herd.

Their eyes met and Michael, his crutches swinging, raced over to the fence near the place where the pony stood. Other ponies milled about, excited in this strange place, anxious with all these people crowding in toward them.

"There she is Gramps, the pony that I saw running along the beach, the one I'm going to bid on."

"It's the same pony that saved you. You two keep crossing paths," Gramps said.

Majesty trotted over to the fence. Michael reached in and rubbed her head. Majesty liked the feeling. "This feels good," she thought. "Keep doing it."

She felt she knew this boy, but she could not remember him. She nuzzled Michael. "Wow," he thought. "She nuzzled me. We were meant for each other."

He could not sleep that night. Oddly, Gramps had a hard time drifting off to sleep, too. Later that night, Gramps saw Michael tossing and turning in his bed.

"You still awake?"

"Yes. I can't forget that pony."

"I haven't seen you this excited in a long time."

"I used to get real excited before my soccer games. Dad would tell me two or three times to get some sleep so I'd have a lot of energy for the game."

"Well, go to sleep so you'll have a lot of energy for the bidding."

"I'm trying."

"Good."

Gramps then fell asleep immediately, but it took a while for Michael to drift off. He dreamed about ponies. And in his dreams Majesty would trot over to him, he would rub her forehead, and she would neigh contentedly.

Michael and Gramps slept late the next morning, although bidders were encouraged to arrive at the carnival grounds before 7 A.M. They showered, grabbed a quick breakfast, and arrived at the carnival where fifty volunteer firefighters were working hard. Their efforts bought Chincoteague the best fire-fighting equipment on the East Coast.

The grounds were filled to overflowing as the auctioneer addressed the crowd on a microphone concerning five foals that had been handpicked by the fire department to be "donated ponies." These ponies would be auctioned off, but donated back to the department to restock their herd. Volunteer firefighters led each pony into the ring, where the auctioneer stood at a podium. Men to either side of him wrote down information. People sat in bleachers, lawn chairs, or folding chairs.

A carnival atmosphere prevailed. Young faces were painted. People munched on spicy crab cakes, traditional clam fritters, hamburgers, and pizza. Games and rides drew all ages. The daring chose the amazing Paratrooper, the exciting Cobra, and the jarring Whip. Others enjoyed Bingo, the "Big Six," the Ferris wheel, the merry-go-round, kiddie cars, and the infamous pirate ship. Many of the people milling around were oblivious to the pony auction, but not Gramps and Michael.

"This sounds like those tobacco auctions that I've seen in the movies and on television, Gramps," Michael said, as they moved to the center of the auction crowd. "I can hardly understand that auctioneer because the bids come so fast."

"Stand on that stump over there, Michael. You can hear better. And put your wallet in your front pocket," Gramps said.

Michael's money, earned from his art prints, was mainly in hundred-dollar bills. Gramps had given him a ten-dollar bill and he had some twenties too.

The crowd parted, Michael pushed over on his crutches, and Gramps lifted him onto the stump. Now he could see Majesty. She appeared to be spooked by the noise and excitement. Amid the turmoil, he recalled the quiet moments last evening when he patted and rubbed her face.

"The prize foal is sold for $1,920," the auctioneer said.

"I hope he's a prize foal," thought Michael. "That's a lot of money."

Majesty was led into the ring. A woman wearing a crimson cowboy hat and a red western outfit with glittering rhinestones turned to her left. "That's the one I like," she told her companion. "Bid on that one." Michael gave Gramps a worried look.

"When the bidding starts, shout out your bid, Michael. I don't want you to lose because the auctioneer can't hear you."

"OK. Thanks."

At that moment Majesty bolted. Two heavy-muscled volunteers quickly settled her down. "That's how I feel too," thought Michael.

"What do I hear? What do I hear? Who'll start the bidding?" With the rush of words and the excitement, anxiety built in Michael. He felt dizzy. Stars flashed in front of his eyes. He thought, "I'm going to faint."

"This is the pony to take home, believe me, trust me. I've got a $400 bid, a $400 bid," yelled the auctioneer. "I need $500."

The words shot out like machine-gun fire. "$500," Michael heard Gramps shout.

"$500. I've got a $500 bid. I need $600. Do I have a $600 bid?" the auctioneer shouted.

"$750," the rhinestone cowgirl bid. Michael looked over at her. "She's probably a rich actress," he thought. "She's beautiful enough." Her beauty frightened him. Beautiful women always got what they wanted in the movies.

"$800," Gramps shouted.

"I've got an $800 bid. I need $900. Do I hear $900?"

"$900," Michael shouted. The strength of his voice surprised him.

"What the . . ?" Gramps said. They both laughed.

The "double bidding" had broken the spell. Michael felt his tension drain away.

"$900. I've got a $900 bid. I need $1,000. Do I have a $1,000 bid?" the auctioneer yelled.

"$1,000," Michael called out. Gramps shook his head. Now Michael was bidding against himself!

"$1,000. I've got a $1,000 bid. Do I have a bid for $1,100?"

"$1,100," said the man with the beautiful woman in red.

"You're doing great," Gramps said. "Keep it up."

Michael looked at Majesty, and he was sure he saw the pony blink. "She winked at me," he thought. "She must be trying to encourage me."

"$1,100. I've got $1,100. I need $1,200, a $1,200 bid," the auctioneer droned.

"$1,200," Michael shouted, his arm raised, his eyes focused on Majesty. "Oh, no," he thought. "I've only got $1,220."

"$1,300."

Then silence. Michael's heart stopped for a second.

"Sold. Sold to the woman in red for $1,300."

Michael couldn't believe his ears. He'd felt sure he'd win. This was the pony of his dreams. He couldn't believe he'd lost. He hadn't felt like this since the accident. The whole thing seemed like a bad dream.

The winning twosome pushed forward through the crowd and disappeared near the podium. Gramps put his hand on Michael's shoulder, but he remained silent for a long while. Then he said, "I'm proud of you. You worked hard to buy a pony. Then you saved that pony's life."

"I choked up," said Michael. "I got off to a lousy start. I was too excited. It takes time to figure these auctions out."

"Try not to be too disappointed."

"I'm real disappointed. That pony and I are supposed to be together."

"Let's go," said Gramps. The heat was getting to him. They left the crowd and sat down; a breeze cooled them. After a minute, Gramps said, "Follow me."

He led Michael around the crowd to the corral where Majesty stood. The rhinestone cowgirl was patting the pony's head. Gramps went up to the woman, tipped his hat, and said, "I'm Donald Larsen. This is my grandson, Michael. We bid against your husband."

"We're not married yet. Mike bought me this beautiful foal to entice me to marry him," she said. "Hi, I'm Susan Sinclair."

"Pleasure to meet you, ma'am."

"Hi," said Michael, wishing he were dead.

"I thought you two were bidding against each other," Susan said, laughing.

"It was my fault," Michael said, frowning. "I got too excited. It wasn't my day."

Majesty came over and nuzzled Michael. A tear ran down Michael's cheek. Gramps patted him on the back. "Sorry," said Michael.

"Tears are nothing to be ashamed of, son," Susan said. "You must love this pony."

"This young man saved your pony for you," Gramps said. "She got her legs ensnarled in fishline and he freed her in the nick of time."

"I saw someone dive off a boat during the swim," said Susan.

"It was a kayak," said Michael.

Gramps told her the whole story. She nodded and said, "Well, it's easy to see why you love this pony. Had I known the story, I would not have bid against you."

"Well, it's over," Gramps said. "Over and done with. Are you in show business, the movies?"

"You could call it show business, but it's not the movies. I'm in the theater," Susan said, laughing. "However, I do live on the West Coast."

Michael's heart sank. The West Coast. He'd never see his beloved pony again.

"Well, honey, how do you like your pony?" the big-boned six-footer said, giving Susan a bear hug and a kiss.

"This is Michael," Susan said. "He saved our pony yesterday," she added, explaining with help from Gramps how Michael had rescued Majesty.

"That's some story," he said. "Oh, by the way, I'm Michael too, Michael Mitchell. Glad to meet you. Call me Mike."

He paused, looked at the downhearted boy on crutches, and said, "What do you want for a reward?"

"I love this pony," said Michael. "I'd like to visit her if you'd let me."

"That's easy enough. I've got a place in Pennsylvania. I'd be happy to have you visit anytime. Susan lives on the West Coast so the pony and I could use some company."

"That's very thoughtful of you," Gramps said. "You'll have a lot of company from us."

"Do you ride, Michael?" Mike said, looking at the young man's crutches.

"Not yet, but I plan to learn," Michael said. "I'd like to learn to ride your pony," he added.

"We can arrange that," Mike said. "Got any ideas for a name? Our pony must have a name."

"I think she's very special. How about Majesty?" said Michael. "That seems like the perfect name for a special pony."

"Majesty it is," said Mike.

When the remaining adult ponies prepared to make the return swim to Assateague, Gramps and Michael sat waiting in their kayak. About sixty ponies waded into the water at Memorial Park and began to swim across the channel to Assateague Island.

"Majesty isn't here, but I wanted to see the return swim anyway," said Michael.

"I'm glad we came," said Gramps. "Stay in the kayak this time."

"I plan to. I like being dry."

The crowds were thinner, the atmosphere casual. A bright sun shone, but much of the drama was gone. Even the ponies seemed more relaxed, though they were eager to return to the peace of their island.

Gramps relaxed in the back of the kayak and let his thoughts drift. Was Michael moving with more assurance and power? Was he depending on his crutches less? Gramps hoped it wasn't his imagination. He and Michael both had great imaginations.

"That was a fine name you picked out for the pony," said Gramps.

"It felt just right. The more I think about it, the more I like it," said Michael. "I think Majesty liked the name, too. She turned to me when I called her Majesty."

The ponies' hooves sank into the mud as they neared the island's banks. One by one they climbed the banks, shook the water from their coats, and disappeared into the marsh as the saltwater cowboys drove them on. Michael wondered if Majesty's harem would miss her. She was gone from them forever.

"Thanks for introducing me to Susan and Mike," Michael said.

"The idea just popped into my mind," said Gramps.

"I felt so bad, so defeated. I just wanted to rush out of there."

"I felt bad too. But I'm like you, Michael, I don't give up easily."

"I can't wait to see Majesty again. I hope Mike has a good home for her. You got his address, right, Gramps?"

"I sure do and the drive to his place isn't that far."

The two paddled, slowly turning the kayak back toward Chincoteague. As their paddles dipped and lifted in unison, man and boy felt the sun on their skin and listened to the distant roar of the surf. They moved easily under the sky's blue dome.

Two months later Gramps pointed the car north and he, Grams, and Michael headed for Mike Mitchell's country place, Majesty's new home.

As they drove, Michael thought about the two good things that came out of his losing bid. "I've invested my money to start my college fund, and I know where Majesty is so I can visit her, thanks to Gramps."

Gramps was silently patting himself on the back for introducing Mike and Michael so his grandson didn't lose contact with Majesty.

Mike's directions were perfect. "Should be right up ahead," said Grams. Soon Gramps turned the steering wheel and the car pulled into a curving driveway lined with long-needled loblolly pines. At its end, a log ranch house combined a colonial appearance with some modern glass and a stunning stone chimney.

"Pretty big place, Gramps."

"Real big," said Grams. "And there are buildings in the woods behind it."

"I bet that's where Majesty is stabled," said Michael.

Moments after the car stopped, Mike opened the front door and walked out to greet them. "Welcome to the home of Majesty and me. I love it and she seems to like it, too."

"I can see why," said Michael. "The house is beautiful, the stable is big, and the woods are perfect for running around."

He paused, smiled, and looked down at his crutches. "Or *walking* around."

"My father built the house and I've always loved it," said Mike. "The drive to work is a long commute, but I'm used to it."

Mike gave them a tour of the house, helped them put their luggage in the guest rooms, and led them to the stable, a freshly painted building with a corral to one side. In it stood an impatient Majesty, who pranced, whinnied, and to everyone's delight, reared.

"That's some welcome," said Mike. "She never greets me like that."

Michael thought of an earlier scene: Majesty on Assateague with her band, surrounded by the endless sky and the pounding surf. "But Majesty doesn't seem to miss it," thought Michael.

"Wow! She remembers me," yelled Michael. His crutches whirled as he raced to the corral fence and reached out to Majesty. She nuzzled his hand, then he patted her head.

"He's always so happy around that pony," Gramps told Mike, who smiled and nodded.

The days passed swiftly as Michael learned to care for Majesty. He cleaned her stall, fed her, and groomed her. Mike showed him some tricks in brushing and combing Majesty's coat; Gramps helped him to maintain his balance while Majesty enjoyed the pampering. The bond between boy and horse strengthened.

When Michael had any extra time, he worked in the yard or helped Grams in the house. "He's a hard worker," said Mike.

"There's not much he can't do when he sets his mind to it," said Gramps. "He's a fighter. He was a pretty fair soccer player before the accident."

Michael learned to operate Mike's power lawn mower and drove it until all of Mike's grass was cut and trimmed for the first time that year. Mike was amazed.

"You know who I want to ride next, Mike," said Michael, sitting on the lawn mower.

"All things in time," Mike answered.

When Mike and Gramps were alone, Mike said, "This visit has been good for everyone—Michael, Majesty, you, Grams, and me. I don't have enough time to keep up this place, spend time with

Majesty, and visit Susan. Grams is a great cook, and you've all been a great help around here. I love this spot, but sometimes it gets a little lonesome."

"I can't thank you enough for your kindness to Michael," said Gramps. "Losing Majesty was a great disappointment to him, but this makes up for it. And Grams and I enjoyed it, too. Had Michael been the winning bidder, we would have had to stable the pony somewhere. I don't know where, and I know we wouldn't have had the money. So thanks from all of us."

On the day Michael was leaving, he and Majesty were inseparable. He combed and brushed the pony as he said good-bye. Gramps helped. Later, with tears in his eyes, Michael said, "Don't worry, Majesty, I'll be back."

As Gramps drove the car home, Michael felt sadder than he had in weeks. "Good-byes are always hard," he thought. Then Gramps broke the silence, saying he had some good news.

"Come next summer, Mike told me he's going to California to visit Susan. He said if we can convince Grams to come again, you can care for Majesty and we'll take care of the house for him."

"Great! I'd love it," said Michael. "In a short time Mike's become a good friend."

"You could cut and trim the lawn," said Gramps.

"I'd take good care of Majesty too. Would you like to go again, Grams?" asked Michael.

"We'll see when the time comes," said Grams. "We'll see."

Winter and spring passed slowly. Grams had not committed herself for a three-week stay at Mike's place in Pennsylvania. "Three weeks, that's a mighty long time," she said.

But Michael had done his homework, helped her around the house, and worked hard at his physical therapy. He was more cheerful at school. He joined in more activities, and he even watched a soccer game. After the team won, the boys dedicated the game to their former star, Michael. He thanked the team, accepted their honor, and didn't cry. Somehow it was easier to watch the game now.

Then the telephone rang. Gramps answered it. "Grams, Mike has to know if we're coming up for three weeks. He's all set to fly out to California the end of June."

Grams hesitated, looked into Michael's worried face, then smiled and said, "Tell him we'll be there with bells on. Get all the details. I'm rarin' to go."

"Hurrah!" shouted Michael, throwing his arms around Grams. "I wish I could call Majesty on the phone."

"Well, you can call Mike," said Grams. "So call him and thank him."

Michael called, thanked Mike, and asked him a hundred questions concerning Majesty. She was healthy, growing, doing well, and, said Mike, "Sometimes I get the impression that she misses you."

"Oh, great!" said Michael.

The first week at Mike's flew by. Majesty and Michael spent all their time together. Susan telephoned and said she was glad that Majesty could spend time with her favorite saltwater cowboy.

"Does rescuing Majesty make me a saltwater cowboy?" Michael asked.

"Sure does," she said.

"I never thought of that," said Michael.

Michael couldn't remember when he had seen Grams and Gramps so happy. Grams started to exercise and lose weight. Sometimes Michael joined her during her morning exercises.

In the stable, Michael had noticed a bridle and saddle with Majesty's name on them. At breakfast, Michael asked Gramps if he had seen them.

"Mike thinks it's about time you learned to ride," said Gramps, "and Majesty's been working with a trainer during our absence."

"Would you help me learn to ride, Gramps? I'd be real careful. There's a wooden platform that would be perfect to help me mount Majesty."

"Mike's already considered everything," thought Gramps.

In the morning, he slowly bridled and saddled Majesty, then moved the wooden platform next to her stirrup. He motioned for Michael to come over.

"Easy, girl," he said, holding Majesty's reins as he helped Michael ease his weight into the saddle. "Whoa, girl."

For a long time Gramps led Majesty around the corral while he held the reins. Michael had spent endless hours in physical therapy, and Gramps didn't want another accident. "Slow and easy," he thought.

Gramps didn't know it, but Michael felt the same way. He felt vulnerable without his crutches. He was like Majesty, accustomed to four points of contact on the ground.

But with Gramps holding the reins and keeping a watchful eye, Majesty first walked, and then moved into a slow trot. Michael was gaining a comfortable feeling in the saddle, shifting his weight this way and that. He was losing his fear of riding.

Dismounting on the wooden platform wasn't easy, but Majesty stood fairly still. Gramps steadied her and helped Michael down. Once on the ground, Michael reached in his pocket and pulled out a sugar lump for Majesty.

Then he patted her, rubbed her down, and groomed her. "I didn't know you knew so much about ponies," Michael told Gramps later.

"I don't. Mike left good instructions and I called Majesty's trainer. He had me practice with him when you were cutting the lawn one day."

"You had me fooled," Michael said.

"Well, Majesty was the key. If she didn't like you so much, it would have been much more difficult. If she had been nervous, I would have stopped right away. I don't want any more accidents."

"I'm feeling more comfortable on Majesty," said Michael. "I loved the trotting after I got used to it."

"My heart was in my throat," Gramps said.

Grams, Gramps, and Michael greeted Mike at the airport when his flight arrived from California. Grams held one hand behind her back and told Mike, "Bend down." Then she slipped a new leather cowboy hat on his head and gave him a kiss.

"Well, what a fine welcome home," Mike said, and he gave Grams a big hug, lifting her off the ground. "You've lost weight."

"Yes," said Grams. "I started exercising again."

"Well, good for you," said Mike. "Gramps will have to keep his eye on you. How's the saltwater cowboy?"

"I'm riding Majesty every day with help from Gramps," said Michael. "I'm beginning to feel right at home in the saddle. But I'm taking it easy."

"Well, that's great news," said Mike. "House-sitting with Majesty at the old Mitchell corral wasn't too bad after all, I take it."

They had a campfire that night. As the flames turned the logs a sparking orange-magenta, Mike told them about Susan and his California adventures, and Michael detailed his riding progress.

"I dreamed about riding Majesty the first time I saw her run past me on the beach," Michael said. "But I didn't think it would happen this quickly. Thanks to you and Gramps it has. And I'm getting better at it. Gramps and I will show you tomorrow."

The stars winked above in the night sky, the fire glowed, and everyone recalled meaningful times in their lives. Gramps said, "I haven't spent a night like this since I was Michael's age."

Grams revealed how difficult it was for Michael's mother to learn the tricks and techniques of horseback riding and how she struggled before she felt at ease in the saddle. Michael thought, "I hope my mother would have been proud of Majesty and me and our attempts to ride together."

"He must have worked hard today," said Mike, as Michael slumbered in his grandmother's lap by the fire. "He's sound asleep. The lawn looks great, so does the garden. I'm going to take some photos to send Susan tomorrow."

"He wanted the place to look good for your homecoming," Gramps said. "He told me he wanted to repay you in some small way for reuniting him with Majesty. It's strange how that pony has brought us all together."

Everyone slept late. Grams made a big breakfast of pancakes, eggs, bacon, toast, oatmeal, orange juice, and coffee. After breakfast, Mike watched Gramps expertly saddle up Majesty.

"You're getting pretty good at that," said Mike.

"Practice makes perfect," said Gramps.

Michael felt a little nervous, but when Majesty looked at him his nervousness left him. He was ready to mount. He climbed his mounting box, handed Mike his crutches, and threw his leg over Majesty in one easy motion without help from Gramps. He took the reins and settled his feet in the stirrups.

Gramps was going to shout "Good boy," but he decided not to at the last second. Michael was concentrating so hard on every action that Gramps didn't want to disturb him. He had never seen Michael appear so sure of himself on Majesty. Michael kicked Majesty gently with his heels. She pranced eagerly from the stable and made a loop, trotting around the corral. Michael rested easily in the saddle, guiding Majesty with the reins.

Grams looked out the window and blinked. Michael was riding Majesty perfectly, sitting erect in the saddle, with the reins resting lightly in his hands. She smiled, then walked to the corral.

Mike was speechless. He never thought Michael would ride this well. Rider and pony continued their harmonious ride moving as one, Majesty responding to Michael's touch on the reins. The pony could sense Michael's new confidence and was aware that the two of them moved together easily.

Gramps was surprised that Michael was not tiring—in fact he seemed to gain strength as he rode. Michael was putting all his skills together for the first time. Grams leaned on a hay bale by the corral and watched in a trance. A tear trickled down her cheek as she thought how pleased Michael's mother would have been.

Michael patted Majesty with one hand as the pony slowed to a walk. Then something happened that no one could explain later. Michael led Majesty toward the wooden mounting box, but she stopped short.

Michael simply nodded, drew up the reins, threw his leg over the saddle, and stepped down. Then he walked over to Gramps. Not carefully, not slowly, not unsurely—he just walked over to Gramps, about fifteen steps. Gramps froze, fearing the boy would fall. Michael handed Gramps the reins, and suddenly he realized what had happened. Mike was holding his crutches, smiling.

"Great ride, Michael," said Mike. "You and Majesty are a great pair. If I hadn't seen it, I would not have believed how well you two move together. As they say, the mystical union of a boy and a pony." He laughed and walked toward Gramps. Michael looked Gramps in the eye and shook his head.

"I walked, Gramps," Michael said. "I walked. I didn't hesitate, or trip, or look for my crutches. I walked. I was so happy that I walked. Majesty and I rode so well together, I forgot about my legs."

Gramps threw his arms around Michael. "What a great moment!" he said. A tear ran down Michael's cheek. Gramps hugged him. Majesty nuzzled them both.

Now Mike was beginning to understand. Michael had walked alone, without crutches, without falling, for the first time since his accident. He had witnessed a triumph. The pony and the boy had produced a miracle. Michael had walked without crutches.

"I don't know what to say," said Mike. "I'm just glad that I'm here to share this moment, this triumph for you and Majesty, Michael."

"Thanks," said Michael. "Sometimes a moment is real special. It changes everything. For me, this moment changed everything."

Grams walked to Michael and hugged him. "I'm just bursting with pride," she said.

"It's just like hitting your first home run," Michael said. "You can't do it every time, but it seems so much easier after the first time."

Michael groomed Majesty, while Mike walked back to the house to phone Susan with the good news. Everyone knew Majesty had helped Michael to walk again.

Michael continued to use his crutches for support as he walked back to the house, but every ten steps or so he would walk a step unassisted. He now knew: he would walk again.

Too soon it was time to leave Mike's place. Mike bought Grams a dozen red roses and Gramps a pipe. Then he said to Michael, "Your gift is visiting Majesty whenever you want. The more, the merrier."

"That's the world's best present," said Michael.

It had been a happy time for everyone. But best of all, Michael had walked. That was the most precious gift. And Majesty helped to give Michael that gift.

The suitcases were packed in the trunk of the car. Gramps had a thermos of coffee next to him in the front seat. Grams had a good book to read. Michael leaned out the window and said, "Thanks for everything, Mike."

"Before you go, I want you to know about a special surprise I have planned for you, Michael," Mike said.

"Another surprise? Too much," said Michael.

"Here it is," said Mike. "In a couple of months I'll call Gramps and we'll all meet at Chincoteague. I'll rent a trailer for Majesty and we'll all ride horses along the beach at Assateague."

"You bring Majesty and we'll be there," said Gramps.

"Count on it," said Michael.

It was a perfect morning at Assateague—a brilliant, cloudless sky, a breeze light enough to move the air gently, and the temperature warm but not hot.

Gramps saddled up Majesty. Mike gave Michael a lift onto Majesty's back. Grams was in the saddle for the first time in thirty years, give or take ten years. Gramps and Mike mounted their ponies and the group set off. The riders headed north along the beach as the surf lapped just beyond the horses' hooves. After a short distance, Michael noticed that Grams looked at home in the saddle. He smiled to himself.

Far off he could see the island curving out to sea as Majesty led the group at a leisurely pace. Michael loved the smell of the salt air, the solitude of the shoreline, the serenity of the island.

The group was alone after passing a few early swimmers. The muffled sound made by the ponies' hooves relaxed the riders. Majesty tossed her head, and memories swept over her. She remembered her parents, Morning Star and Bright Star, and the stallion who killed her father, Devil Chaser. She recalled the harem and the quiet life by the sea.

Then she heard a loud whinny and recognized it from her distant memory. It was Black Thunder. She visualized him trotting next to her. He lifted his hooves high and tossed his mane. "You have fulfilled your destiny," he said. Then the vision faded.

Majesty broke into a frisky trot, surprising Michael. She was moving faster, but in a smooth, easy way. Michael thought, "It's because she's happy." And he realized that he was happy too.

He was perfectly happy riding Majesty under this magnificent sky, with the sea on one side and the island's dunes and marsh grass on the other. Then he spotted a harem grazing contentedly off in the distance.

The stallion looked up as they rode past. Majesty looked at the grazing ponies and recognized Devil Chaser. He was older, and he moved more slowly. She could just discern a scar on one shoulder. Had he battled a young stallion for the harem? Or was it a scar from battling Bright Star?

Devil Chaser watched the ponies and riders moving north along the beach. For a second he thought he recognized the mare in the lead. But no, she had disappeared. The memory faded, and he dropped his head and continued grazing.

Mike trotted his horse forward, then rode alongside Michael. "You two ride well together," he said.

"I feel it too," said Michael. "This is the only pony I've ever ridden, but we seem to sense each other's next move, which makes it easy for me to ride. And my legs are finally getting stronger."

"You've had a long battle," Mike said.

"Sometimes it has been tough," Michael said. "But Majesty gave me hope, gave me the will to go on. Now I feel like the hardest part is over."

As Michael and Mike chatted, a great contentment swept over Majesty. She felt she could follow this endless sea forever. The day was perfect.

Grams and Gramps rode behind, enjoying the day and the sea. "I didn't realize that you were such a good rider," said Gramps.

"I did some riding when our daughter took lessons," said Grams. "You're not so bad yourself."

"Majesty's trainer gave me some tips," Gramps said. "I feel we've come a long way since Michael first saw that pony Majesty."

"Yes, we have," said Grams. "But not half as far as Michael. He's a new boy. He's accomplished so much."

"Sometimes life throws a curve ball," said Gramps. "Something that we don't expect."

Mike slowed his horse and dropped back, leaving Michael and Majesty up ahead.

Michael leaned forward in the saddle and said to Majesty, "On a day like this I could ride forever. How about you?" Majesty tossed her head and set a steady pace for the riders as they moved northward along the beach.

## Chincoteague Pony Swim, Pony Penning, and Auction

Though no one is sure how the ponies came to Assateague Island, the place has been home to two herds of wild ponies—one in Maryland and one in Virginia—for about three hundred years. The most popular legend suggests that the ponies' ancestors swam ashore from a sinking Spanish ship. Some people think pirate ships brought the ponies. Another story says the ponies are simply descended from horses that belonged to early settlers who sent their animals to graze on the island.

In Virginia, the herd is managed by the Chincoteague Volunteer Fire Company. (The town of Chincoteague is on the island of Chincoteague, which is located next to Assateague.) According to a permit issued by the United States Fish and Wildlife Service, the Fire Company can keep 150 ponies in the Chincoteague National Wildlife Refuge, part of Assateague Island.

In order to limit the size of the herd, the Fire Company sells some of the ponies every summer. Starting on the last Wednesday in July, a number of the younger ponies are offered for sale at an event that has become world famous—the Chincoteague Pony Swim, Pony Penning, and Auction. Many lucky bidders take home one of the ponies. At the same time, the proceeds of the sale benefit the Fire Company.

The idea of an auction may be based in history, as owners annually rounded up livestock on both Assateague and Chincoteague Islands to brand or harness them.

In order for the ponies to come to the auction, they must swim across a channel to the site on Chincoteague Island where the sale takes place. "Saltwater cowboys" (firemen and their friends) herd the ponies together and guide them as they swim across the narrowest part of the channel between the two islands. After resting a while, the ponies are moved to the corral where the auction is held the next day. The auction itself is an exciting time for everyone—those bidding on the ponies and those who are only watching.

On the day after the auction, the remaining ponies will make the return swim to the wildlife refuge. Both swims are planned for the time of low tide, when the current in the channel is either not moving at all or else is moving very slowly. Veterinarians are on hand to check the ponies before and after the swims. The ponies are also checked from time to time during the year, as the Fire Company wants to be sure that the herd stays healthy.

The auction with its related activities has proved to be a very good source of funds for the Fire Company. In 2003, the average price of a pony was almost $1,800, and seventy-two ponies were sold.